J

A2170 701513 2

THE ART OF TIME TRAVEL

QUEEN OF JAZZ

GET ELLA TO THE APOLLO

NEW YORK 1934 NEW YORK

CHILDREN'S LIBRARY

∞ BY LISA AND JOHN MULLARKEY ∞
ILLUSTRATED BY COURTNEY BERNARD

Calico

An Imprint of Magic Wagon
www.abdopublishing.com

To Ted Petitt: We know you're in the
front row listening to Ella and Frank.
—Lisa & John

www.abdopublishing.com

Published by Magic Wagon, a division of ABDO, PO Box 398166, Minneapolis,
Minnesota 55439. Copyright © 2015 by Abdo Consulting Group, Inc.
International copyrights reserved in all countries. No part of this book may
be reproduced in any form without written permission from the publisher.
Calico™ is a trademark and logo of Magic Wagon.

Printed in the United States of America, North Mankato, Minnesota.
102014
012015

**THIS BOOK CONTAINS
RECYCLED MATERIALS**

Written by Lisa and John Mullarkey
Illustrated by Courtney Bernard
Edited by Tamara L. Britton and Bridget O'Brien
Cover and interior design by Candice Keimig

Library of Congress Cataloging-in-Publication Data

Mullarkey, Lisa, author.
   Get Ella to the Apollo / by Lisa and John Mullarkey ; illustrated by Courtney
Bernard.
      pages cm. -- (The art of time travel)
   Summary: Thirteen-year-old Chloe and her younger brother Parker are
transported back to 1934 Harlem where they meet Ella Fitzgerald the day before
she wins Amateur Night at the Apollo, but with Ella making plans to miss the
event, the kids have to get her to the Apollo, and convince her to sing instead of
dance.
   ISBN 978-1-62402-087-2
1. Fitzgerald, Ella--Juvenile fiction. 2. Apollo Theater (New York, N.Y. : 125th
Street)--Juvenile fiction. 3. Jazz singers--Juvenile fiction. 4. Time travel--
Juvenile fiction. 5. Brothers and sisters--Juvenile fiction. 6. Harlem (New York,
N.Y.)--History--Juvenile fiction. [1. Fitzgerald, Ella--Fiction. 2. Apollo Theater
(New York, N.Y. : 125th Street)--Fiction. 3. Singers--Fiction. 4. Time travel--
Fiction. 5. Brothers and sisters--Fiction. 6. Harlem (New York, N.Y.)--History-
-20th century--Fiction. 7. New York (N.Y.)--History--1898-1951--Fiction.] I.
Mullarkey, John, author. II. Bernard, Courtney, illustrator. III. Title.
   PZ7.M91148Ge 2015
   813.6--dc23
                                        2014031663

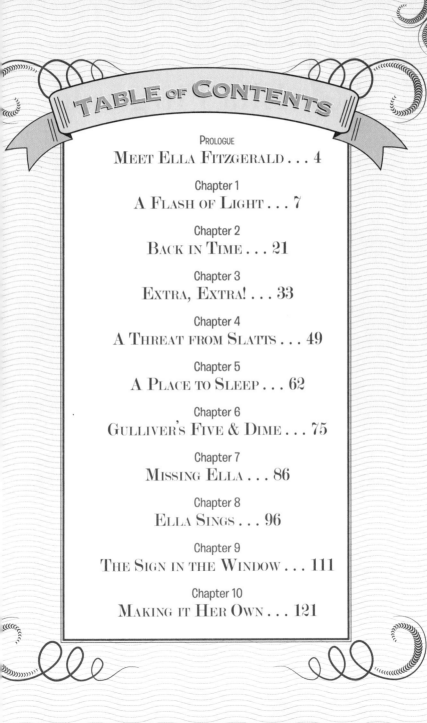

TABLE of CONTENTS

Meet **Ella Fitzgerald**

—➤❋◄—

Ella Fitzgerald is one of the greatest female jazz singers of all time. Known as the "First Lady of Jazz," she won thirteen Grammy Awards and sold over forty million albums during a career that lasted more than half a century.

Ella was born in Newport News, Virginia, on April 15, 1917. Her parents divorced shortly after she was born. She and her mother moved to Yonkers, New York. After her mother died in 1932, Ella ended up in Harlem, homeless during the Great Depression.

Despite the hard times, Ella believed she would find success doing what she loved most: dancing and singing. She scraped together money to visit venues such as the Savoy Ballroom, the Harlem Opera House, the Cotton Club, and the Apollo Theater.

On November 21, 1934, 17-year-old Ella performed at the Apollo Theater's Amateur Night. She showed up with unkempt hair, a ratty dress, and men's boots on her feet. She also needed a bath.

Ella had planned to dance. But at the last minute, she decided to sing instead. This decision was the pivotal moment in her life and career.

Ella won the competition. But because of her appearance, the accompanying week-long singing gig wasn't offered to her.

However, Ella impressed Apollo band member Benny Carter. He introduced her to important people in the music business. She was soon offered a weekly gig with the Tiny Bradshaw Band where she met her mentor Chick Webb. Four years later, her recording of "A-Tisket, A-Tasket" was a number one hit.

Ella belonged on the stage and was a natural performer. She gained advice from, and later worked with, famous jazz musicians including Duke Ellington, Billie Holiday, and Louis Armstrong.

Ella Fitzgerald died on June 15, 1996. The rough-and-tumble girl who was once living on the streets of Harlem accomplished her dream and left a lasting impression on everyone who has ever heard her sing.

A FLASH OF LIGHT

"You can't be serious, Chloe," said Parker as he slammed the car door. "On my birthday, I took you to the water park. This is the thanks I get?"

"You're eleven." I pinched his freckled cheek. "I'm thirteen. I picked something more mature this time."

"Great. Just great," he said as he kicked a pebble. "Jazz festivals are boring."

I sighed. "Don't be such a party pooper."

Mom ignored us as she bopped her head to the rhythm that floated through the air. She gave me a thumbs up. "Now that's music to my ears."

"Not mine," said Parker.

"Stop complaining," I said. "My birthday. My choice."

Mom agreed. "It's one afternoon. Besides, your

friends are bound to show up with a football soon."

"Not soon enough," he mumbled.

As much as Mom and I loved jazz, Parker despised it. Unless there was an electric guitar riff involved, he wouldn't listen to it.

Mom picked up her chair and picnic basket and led the way toward the Green. We dodged parents pushing strollers and clowns twisting balloons into animal shapes as we weaved in and out of the crowds.

Parker stomped along, glaring at everything we passed. "Why is it so packed?"

"Because it's a beautiful July day," said Mom. "It's not often that New Jersey gets a day without humidity smack in the middle of summer. Who wouldn't want to come out and enjoy a perfect day filled with music?" She winked at me. "Jazz music."

Parker clenched his jaw. "But we came here last year, too. Why does this stupid town always have these boring jazz festivals?"

"First of all, Bakersfield isn't a stupid town," said

Mom. "Back in the 1930s and '40s, jazz acts came here to try out new music in front of a live audience before opening up in New York City. Bakersfield is so close to the city that it was the perfect pit stop for them."

"Mom's right," I said. "In music class, we learned that if someone famous went to the Apollo Theater or to the Harlem Opera House, you could bet they came here, too."

Parker wasn't listening. He was much more interested in the food trucks selling candy apples and funnel cakes.

"At least the food smells good," he said. He licked his lips. "I'm starving."

I laughed. When wasn't he hungry? For such a super skinny fifth grader, he sure did stuff his face a lot.

Mom held up the picnic basket. "This will put some meat on your bones. After we eat our sandwiches, you can get some treats." Then she motioned toward the Green and dropped her bag onto the grass. "Since I can see the stage's red, white, and blue bunting through those trees, I'm setting up camp here. We're close enough to hear everything but far enough away that the speakers won't hurt our ears."

I spread out our blanket. "This is a perfect spot." Just then, a woman started to sing on the stage. "She sounds like Ella Fitzgerald! Doesn't she?"

Mom shrugged. "Sort of. But there isn't really anyone on the planet that sounds *exactly* like Ella. No one has a voice as smooth as hers. No one."

"No one," Parker mimicked.

Mom dug through her bag and pulled out a white envelope with *Happy Birthday, Chloe* written on it. "This festival's free." She handed it to me. "This is your gift."

I tore the envelope open and gasped.

"What is it?" asked Parker. "Money?"

"No way!" I shouted, as I jumped up and down. "It's tickets to the Apollo Theater. *The Apollo Theater*!"

Parker's eyes lit up. "Is that the new movie theater they built at the mall?"

I giggled.

"Nope," said Mom. "It's not a movie theater. It's a music hall in Harlem, New York, where Ella Fitzgerald got her start. You can see a concert there, attend a lecture, or take a tour. I've wanted to go ever since I was in high school."

Parker didn't seem too impressed.

"I got an extra ticket," said Mom.

"Come with us," I said to Parker. "All of the great jazz artists have performed there. Right, Mom?"

She nodded as she slathered sunscreen on her legs. "Anyone who was someone played at the Apollo at one time or another."

"Like Ella!" I shouted. "She sure was someone. They called her the First Lady of Jazz."

Parker rolled his eyes. "What's so great about Ella Fitzgerald?"

"What's so great about her?" I asked. Was he

kidding? Even though Parker wasn't into jazz music, he knew that Ella Fitzgerald was my all-time favorite singer. After two book reports on her, I considered myself sort of an Ella expert. I loved her music so much that I named our dog, Fitz, after her.

"Ella only had to hear a song once before she could mimic and remember the melody and rhythm," I said. "She couldn't always remember the words though. But that's the coolest part. She replaced words with rhythmic sounds that resembled instruments."

Mom nodded. "It's called scat singing. Ella was a natural. She was a good dancer, too."

"Not a good dancer," I protested. "A great dancer."

Mom smiled. "We're going to Amateur Night."

I slapped my cheek and fanned myself with the tickets. "I think I'm gonna faint. This is the best birthday ever."

Parker yawned. "What's Amateur Night?"

"It's a competition where regular people, amateurs, get a chance to perform and win money," said Mom.

"It takes place every Wednesday night. Long before those reality shows popped up on television, there was Amateur Night at the Apollo." She tossed the sunscreen to me. "Can you believe we're actually going to see where Ella sang in front of an audience for the first time?"

"When was that?" Parker asked. "A million years ago?"

"Nope," I said. "In 1934."

"And after all these years, they still have the same rules," said Mom. "If the crowd doesn't like you, they'll boo you right off the stage."

"But Ella never got booed off," I said. "Ever."

Parker put his hands over his ears. "Ella, Ella, Ella."

I stuck my tongue out at him.

He tossed the football to me. "I have to go to the bathroom." He glanced over at the Porta-Potty. "Come with me."

"No way. Gross. Never gonna happen."

"Go," said Mom. "Please?"

Parker smirked and pulled me off my blanket.

"Fine," I said "But there's no way we're using a Porta-Potty." I waved my fingers in front of my nose. "I know where there's a bathroom we can use."

Two minutes later, we were standing outside of a tall brick building. I pulled the door open and bowed. "Welcome to the Bakersfield Historical Society."

He groaned. "Isn't this the place with all that music stuff? I'd rather use the Porta-Potty."

The Bakersfield Historical Society was a museum. My sixth grade class visited in June and I still hadn't stopped talking about the jazz exhibit.

I shoved him inside. "Just use the bathroom and then we'll go. Promise."

Once inside, it took my eyes a minute to adjust to the darkness. Parker went into the men's room.

"It smells like dirty feet in here, doesn't it?" asked Parker when he returned. He sniffed the air. "More like dirty diapers."

"It's the old newspapers," I said as I tapped on the wall. "These are posters of all the jazz greats that performed in Bakersfield." There were at least two dozen on the wall. "They were some of the best singers and musicians in the world." My favorites were of Benny Goodman, Count Basie with his Orchestra, and, of course, Ella.

Then I dragged him over to a different wall. "This trumpet belonged to Dizzy Gillespie!"

"Dizzy? What kind of name is Dizzy?"

I raised my eyebrows. "What kind of name is Parker?"

Parker scrunched his nose. Then he walked over to the album covers framed in black. "These are signed by the artists. I bet they're worth a lot of money."

Then I showed him sheet music signed by Louis Armstrong. "This is very valuable. Probably worth at least a million bucks."

His eyes opened wide. "Really?"

I nodded. Then I whipped out my cell phone and

started snapping pictures. "But I've saved the best for last." I led him to the far corner of the room. There on a small shelf, was a faded purple pillbox hat. "Ta-da!"

"It's just an ugly hat," said Parker, sounding disappointed.

"Just an ugly hat? It's the hat that Ella wore in the 1930s and '40s. There are a lot of pictures of her wearing it." I scanned the wall. "Look! She's wearing it in this picture."

Parker stood on his tiptoes to get a better look. "How much is it worth?"

"It was Ella's," I said. "It's priceless."

"It sure doesn't look like it's worth anything," he said. "Was that picture taken in Bakersfield?"

I read the sign under it. "Taken outside of Gulliver's Five & Dime in Harlem, New York, during the Great Depression. Note the sign hanging in the window." I took a picture of the photo.

"The sign in the window says No Colored." I folded my arms. "Well, I'd never go in there. Can you imagine if we still had signs like that? Maybe that's why Ella's standing outside of the store. She's not allowed to go inside."

Suddenly, the hat fell off the shelf.

Parker and I jumped back and stared at it.

Finally, he picked it up off the floor. "How did that happen? Are we going to get in trouble?"

I took the hat out of his hand. "We didn't do anything wrong." I gently placed the hat on my head. "It fits," I whispered. I closed my eyes and pretended I had a microphone in my hand. "A-tisket, a-tasket, a green and yellow basket . . ."

"Put it back," barked Parker. "You're going to get in trouble."

But I didn't care. I sang some more.

"There's somebody I'm longing to see
I hope that it turns out to be
Someone who'll watch over me . . ."

When I finished, Parker clapped.

"If only I could have met Ella," I said.

"It's your birthday. Make a wish," he said. "Birthday wishes always come true."

I pushed my bangs out of my eyes. "She died a long time ago. I can't meet her."

"Now who's being a party pooper? Just make the wish."

"Okay," I said as I squeezed my eyes shut. "I wish I could meet the one and only Ella Fitzgerald."

Just then, a strange tingling sensation shot through my body. When I opened my eyes, there was a flash of light. It was as if someone snapped a picture. Then the hat started to shake on my head. Before long, the whole room shook.

"What's happening?" I asked. "Are we having an earthquake?"

There was a brighter flash.

Parker shielded his eyes. "I don't know." He tried to swipe the hat off my head. "It won't budge."

I reached up. "It's stuck!" No matter how hard I

pulled, it wouldn't move. It was stuck fast.

The lights suddenly dimmed and a cool drifty breeze whooshed past us. The whole room started to spin. Some of the posters crashed to the floor.

"Run," I screamed. "Run!"

Parker grabbed my hand and pulled me toward the door. "The knob won't turn. I can't open it."

The room grew dimmer and the air became cooler.

"Hurry," I whispered. "Push harder."

Parker rammed his shoulder into the door and as it opened, we stumbled out and fell into a heap on the sidewalk.

"Chloe," said Parker quietly. "I feel dizzy. I'm getting this . . ."

"Weird feeling?" I asked.

Parker sat up. "Yeah. Like we're not in Bakersfield anymore."

BACK IN TIME

"Ha, ha. Very funny," I said as I stood and pulled him up with me. I dusted off my shorts.

I felt woozy. Sort of like I'd just gotten off a roller coaster and my legs were still rubbery. I grabbed the railing to steady myself. "What was that flash? Did you have your cell phone out?"

Parker patted his pocket. "My phone's dead. I forgot to charge it. Maybe it was your phone?"

I pulled it out of my pocket. "I thought I turned it off earlier." I slid the bar over to the right. The phone lit up.

"It's not working. Every time I touch Mom's number, nothing happens. I even tried dialing with the keypad. No texting either."

"You tried to call Mom?"

I nodded. "I feel like we've been gone for a while. I want to tell her we're on our way back." I tilted my ear into the air. "Do you hear that?"

"Hear what?" he asked. Just then, he covered his ears as a loud honking filled the air. "I think the whole world hears that honking."

"No. Not the cars. What don't you hear?"

He shrugged.

"Jazz," I said. "Why can't we hear the music from the festival anymore?" I put a finger in my ear and wiggled it around. Everything felt strange. The kind of strange feeling you get when you wake up from a deep sleep.

Parker poked my arm. "Turn around slowly and look up."

And that's when I saw that there were stairs that led up to the street. The purple pillbox hat was laying on the first step.

Parker bent down and carefully picked it up. "I guess it finally came off." He tossed it to me then stood on the first step. "I don't remember walking down any stairs to get to the building. Do you?" I pushed him in front of me. "Nope. That's why you're going first." I followed him up the steps to what I thought would be State Street. But when I got to the last step and looked out, I knew we weren't anywhere near there.

There were tall buildings surrounding us. Taller than any building in Bakersfield. The sidewalk was wider and it sloped down to a busy street. Car horns blared and the smell of burning wood filled the air.

Parker's voice cracked as he looked up into the chalky, gray sky. "I'm not sure where we are."

Before I could say anything, a large man pushing a cart of laundry bags knocked into me.

"Hey, move outta the way," he yelled as he steered the cart around me. "Why ya standin' there lookin' up at the sky?" He stopped and stared at us. "Where'd you get those clothes and shoes? The circus?"

We quickly scanned the area.

I scratched my head. "Parker, I'm really confused. I don't remember reading anything about antique cars and trucks being on display. Is this part of the festival?"

"I guess so." He scrunched his nose. "What's that burning smell?"

I pointed to the street corner. A bunch of people were huddled around a garbage can. Flames licked up from inside the can. People jostled each other trying to stay close to it and keep warm.

"I don't know what happened back at the historical society but I'm starting to think that we're not in Bakersfield anymore."

Parker looked pale. "It's cold, too. So much for the nice July day."

We walked toward the street corner. It looked different from the street corners at home. The lampposts were old-fashioned like the ones you'd see in the movies. A police officer used a whistle to direct traffic. The street sign was marked Lenox Avenue on one side and 123rd Street on the other. "We're lost," I said.

"Which way do you think the Green is?" asked Parker looking from left to right several times. "Should we just ask someone?"

I wanted to tell Parker that I didn't think we'd ever find the Green around here but before I could, a small boy shouted at us.

"Get your papers here!" yelled the boy. "Afternoon edition. Read all about it!"

I dragged Parker to the other side of the sidewalk. "Maybe he'll know."

But before we could ask, a large, black woman rushed by us. She kept looking back over her shoulder as she hummed and sang parts of a song. She stopped at the corner, looked around for a minute, then rushed back past us and ducked behind a car.

Her hair was a mess and she had on an oversized green sweater and a gray flannel skirt that was frayed on the bottom. She was definitely trying to hide from someone. But she also seemed to have a song on her mind. After running back and forth for a few minutes, she stopped in front of me.

"You ain't seen Slatts 'round here, have you?" she asked, out of breath.

I shook my head. "We don't know anyone named Slatts."

"Who is he?" asked Parker. "We're not from around here."

The woman stared at us with her mouth half open and her eyebrows raised high. "You don't know Slatts? Everyone 'round here knows Slatts." Then she leaned in and whispered. "If you don't know Slatts, chances are he knows you and will be payin' you a visit real soon." She flung her hand in the air. "He's about this tall and this round." She bent over and laughed. "Fat as can be. In fact, he's so fat you kids could roll him down this here sidewalk. He dresses mighty fine though."

He sounded like a clown. "I'd know if we saw

someone that looked like that, ma'am," I said. "We definitely haven't seen Slatts."

"Did you just call me ma'am?" she asked.

I nodded.

She let out a hoot and a howl and slapped her thigh. "Well, I'll be." Then she turned serious. "Don't call me ma'am again. My friends all call me Ella." Then she noticed the pillbox hat in my hand and grabbed it. "Where did you find that? I've been lookin' high and low for it." She tossed it on the ground.

My heart raced. Ella? Was this the Ella Fitzgerald? It couldn't be! I studied her face. It sort of looks like her. But it couldn't be, could it?

Then Ella closed her eyes and stood perfectly still.

"Is she okay?" asked Parker after a minute. "What's she doing?"

I shrugged. "You don't think she could be . . ."

"What?" asked Parker.

"Never mind," I said. My cheeks felt hot. It must be someone dressed up for the festival.

"Look at her hair," whispered Parker. "Have you ever seen someone's hair so knotted?"

My heart raced. Ella's hair was always a mess. Every book I had ever read mentioned her uncombed hair.

She stood perfectly still for another minute. I was just about to ask her if she was all right when she opened her mouth and started to sing.

She sang softly at first. People rushed past her but no one paid much attention. But as her singing grew louder, people slowed down and crowded around us. The louder she sang, the more people stopped and stared. Then, one person threw a coin into her hat. Then another and another. As her singing became more upbeat, she began to clap her hands and swing her hips.

"She has the most beautiful voice I've ever heard," I said. It just had to be Ella.

Parker agreed. "And she's got some great dance moves, too."

I closed my eyes and swayed back and forth as her sweet voice floated through the air. Although I didn't

recognize the song, she really sounded an awful lot like Ella Fitzgerald.

But no sooner had she started singing, she stopped. She turned toward me and whispered, "Lord, help me. Slatts is here."

I looked around but didn't see anyone that looked like Slatts. But when I turned to tell her, she was already climbing into the back of an oversized tan car. I picked up her pillbox hat and as I went to lean in the car to give it to her, a large thick hand grabbed it and then slammed the door. The car screeched away.

"Where is she going in such a rush?" I asked Parker. "And who was she?"

"Who cares! You just gave away the only thing we have that links us back to Bakersfield."

I covered my face with my hands. "What was I thinking? I promise I'll get the hat back."

He clenched his fists. "Face it, Chloe. You blew it." He turned his back to me and tried to get my cell phone to work.

"Get your papers here!" the boy shouted again. "Read all about it! Only a nickel."

"Excuse me," I said. "Can you tell me where we are? I think we're lost."

"Got a nickel?" he asked in between his shouting.

I sighed. "No."

The boy shrugged. "No nickel. No paper."

The boy had on a wool cap that was pulled down low. His sweater was ripped and his pants were too big. His shoes were worn out and it looked like he only had one sock on.

"Aren't you too young to sell newspapers?" I asked. He couldn't be older than six or seven. "Where's your mom?"

The boy was too busy collecting nickels to answer.

I noticed a stack of newspapers behind his feet. I bent over to take a peek and blinked hard when I saw the date. I looked again just to be sure.

"Parker," I said as my voice trembled. "Tell me I'm not dreaming."

"Okay," said Parker, smiling. "You're not dreaming."

But when I held the paper up, his smile faded as he read aloud. "*The New York Times*. November 20, 1934." His face turned white. "November 20, 1934."

"Now we know we're definitely not in New Jersey anymore," I said. "And it's November? I don't know how or why, but we've obviously traveled back in time to 1934. But where exactly are we?"

Parker folded his arms. "I can't figure out why we came back in time or how we got here, but I know one thing for sure. We're in New York City. Harlem. We're smack in the middle of the Great Depression!"

"How do you know?" I asked. "Are you sure?"

"I'm positive," said Parker. Then he pointed to a building behind us.

When I looked, I was staring at the same Gulliver's Five & Dime store we saw in the picture at the historical society. That's when I knew for sure. I gasped and clutched my chest. "Parker. My wish came true! We just met the one and only Ella Fitzgerald."

EXTRA, EXTRA!

"Ella Fitzgerald?" said Parker. "The *real* Ella Fitzgerald?" His voice cracked. "Are you sure?"

"It has to be her. Like Mom said, there's no one else in the world who has her smooth voice. She said her name was Ella! It makes sense. We know we're in Harlem. She said the hat was hers, too."

Parker started to cry. "We have to find a way back to Bakersfield." He looked up at the sky. "It'll be dark in a few hours." He shivered. "I'm cold. And afraid."

We needed to find some warmer clothes. Shorts and T-shirts were July weather clothes.

I rubbed his back and arms to warm him up. "If we were able to get here, there has to be a way back, too."

But secretly I wasn't so sure.

Parker rubbed his eyes. "Someone just came out of Gulliver's. He's coming this way."

A tall man stepped out of the store and quickly walked toward us.

He rushed up to the newspaper boy as he waved a broom. "You can't be selling papers here. Slatts knows I sell them in my store. We have an agreement."

The boy frowned. "Slatts sent me here, Mr. Gulliver. Said to sell them in front of your store."

Mr. Gulliver's nostrils flared. "Tell Slatts I pay my money. He gets his share. It may be late sometimes but he gets it."

The boy reached in his pocket and pulled out a piece of paper. "Got a message for ya. Slatts gave it to me himself."

Mr. Gulliver grabbed the note and read it aloud. "Pay up." He crumpled the note and tossed it into the street.

The boy continued selling his papers.

Mr. Gulliver pulled out a handkerchief and

dabbed his face. That's when he noticed Parker and I standing there.

"You know that woman you were talking to?" he asked. "The large black woman?"

Parker nodded.

"If you see her again, tell her to stay away from Gulliver's, will you? Tell her I said to stay clear away from my place. It's for her own good. Got it?"

I jumped up. "But we'd never tell anyone to stay away from any store. The color of a person's skin shouldn't . . ."

"Move along," came a gruff voice from behind me. I turned around and came face to face with a police officer. "You hear me, missy?" he said as he poked my shoulder with his billy club. "Move along now. This is my beat. I don't want any trouble from anyone."

"I'm not doing anything wrong," I said. The police officer shook his head. Out of the corner of my eye, I could see Mr. Gulliver making his way into his store.

That's when Parker swooped in and grabbed my

elbow. "Sorry officer. My sister isn't feeling well."

Parker pulled me down the sidewalk and pushed me into an alley. "Are you crazy? The last thing we need is to get arrested. He could have thrown you in jail. Then how would we ever get back home?" His voice lowered. "Mom always says not to look for trouble."

I rubbed my elbow. "I was just trying to tell Mr. Gulliver . . ."

"I know what you were trying to do. But we can't change the way Mr. Gulliver thinks. We know he doesn't like black people. But don't you think we have more important things to worry about now?" His voice cracked.

We walked a few blocks without talking. Neither of us knew where we were going but it felt better to walk somewhere than to just sit around waiting for something to happen. Finally, I saw a sign hanging on a lamppost: Historical Society 335 125th Street. "Let's go," I said. "It's a historical society. That's how we got into this mess. Maybe that's how we're going to get out of it, too."

"But it's not the same one," said Parker. "Will it work?"

"Who knows," I said. "But it's worth a try. Unless . . ."

"Unless what?"

"Unless you want to spend the rest of your life in Harlem."

We walked quickly down the sloped street and made our way to 125th Street. "Here it is," said Parker, as we stood in front of a run-down building. The sign said New Amsterdam Old Dutch Historical Society. "This doesn't look like the ticket back to Bakersfield."

"Sh," I said. "Do you hear that?" I held my ear to the door. "Music!" I opened the door. A young woman sat on a bench in a small lobby. Dusty bookcases lined the walls. Historic maps of New York hung on the wall behind the bench. A table in the center of the room held an empty plate with crumbs on it.

The woman yawned. "You ain't seen Slatts out there, did you?"

Parker shook his head. "Slatts sure does get around. Why does everyone want to know where he is?"

The woman rushed over to the door and shut it behind us. "Slatts can't find her here. He dropped her off on Seventh Avenue. Thinks she's running numbers." She locked the door. "If he knows she's wasting time singing and dancing, he'll pitch a fit." She looked us over. "No one wants to witness one of his crazy outbursts."

I looked around the place. "Who did he drop off?"

"Ella," said the woman pointing to a figure dancing in the next room.

I grabbed Parker's arm and squeezed it tight. "OMG! It's *her*. The Queen of Jazz!" My knees felt weak. I held out my arm. "Pinch me."

"Calm down," said Parker. "She's just a person."

"Just a person? That's like saying Abraham Lincoln was just another guy." I pushed past him and walked up to Ella. I thrust my hand into hers. "I'm your biggest fan. My mom and I love listening to your records."

Ella backed up a few inches. "You again?" She shook her head. "What are you talkin' 'bout?"

"You're the great Ella Fitzgerald, aren't you?"

Her friend got a good laugh out of that. "Ella? Great? Raggedy and poor as can be, yes. Great?" She winked at Ella. "I suppose Slatts thinks you're great. He's sweet on you."

I started to talk but Parker covered my mouth with his hand. "Remember," he whispered. "We're not supposed to know about the future."

Ella hummed as she walked to the window and peeked through the curtains. "I gotta eat. My belly's been growlin' all day."

"We haven't eaten either," I said. "Maybe we can go out to dinner. Do you have any money, Parker?"

Ella laughed. "We don't need money to eat 'round here. We don't go out to dinner much either. That's for rich folk and there ain't many of them 'round here no more." She looked around the room. "That's why we came here. Sometimes the society puts out a platter of cookies and punch for the visitors. But, today isn't one of those days. Barely a crumb to be found." Then she turned toward her friend. "Last time we went out to dinner, we went fishin' in a garbage can, didn't we?"

Parker has always had impeccable timing. Because right then and there, his stomach roared like a lion.

"Honey," she said. "Let's give that belly a rest. I know where we can get something to eat. You two kids sure seem friendly enough." Then her eyes lit up. "You gave me back my hat. That makes us friends already. Feel like joinin' me and eatin' for free?"

"Will the food be from a garbage can?" Parker asked.

I jabbed Parker in the rib. "Don't be so rude."

Ella studied us. "This is your lucky day. There is free food at the church tonight. Tomorrow may be chicken bones from the garbage but tonight, we feast!"

Parker whispered, "Shouldn't we be searching for a way back to Bakersfield?"

Parker was right, but when would I ever have the chance to talk to my hero again? "We'll eat fast."

Parker folded his arms and sighed.

"Promise."

He leaned into my ear. "Why can't we go to her house for dinner? Maybe her mom could help us." He rubbed his stomach.

"Because she's homeless. She doesn't have a house. Or a mom."

Parker looked shocked. "How old is she?"

"She's only seventeen. Her mother died when she was fifteen. She lived with an aunt for a while but ran away. She lives with anyone who'll take her in. I remember reading that she had lots of friends. Good friends and some not-so-good friends. I guess Slatts is one of the not-so-good ones."

Ella opened the door a crack.

"Any sign of Slatts?" asked Parker.

Ella threw back her head and laughed. "I like you. You're a quick study. Slatts should be busy tonight. If he knew I wasn't runnin' numbers for him, he'd be sore."

"What's runnin' numbers?" I said.

"Yeah, runnin' numbers," said Ella. "Folks place bets in a lottery and pick numbers to match horse racing results. Slatts is in charge of the local lottery. I collect the bettin' slips from the folks and bring them to him." She held up a few slips. "He ain't all that bad. As long as I do what he says when he says, I'll be okay. It's just somethin' I gotta do."

Ella's friend agreed. "Sometimes you gotta do whatever you can to make money. Everyone needs money, you know."

"Ella doesn't," I said. "She's a rich woman. At least, she will be soon." Then I faced Ella. "You're going to be rich! Richer than rich. You're going to have number one records and sing with all the great jazz singers. You'll even make an album with Louis Armstrong!"

"Louis Armstrong is one of my heroes," said Ella as she fanned herself. "That would be a dream." Then she puffed her cheeks. "You escape from someplace? Got a fever? You talkin' nonsense, girl. I'm leavin' for Chicago with Slatts tomorrow night. He says I won't have to run numbers or worry myself about money anymore. Says I'll be respectable. Maybe give dance lessons. I sure love to dance and could show you both how to do the shimmy or the Lindy Hop. Watch this . . ."

All of the sudden, as if she turned on a switch, Ella moved her feet. She stomped and tapped across the old wooden floor. She stopped on a dime, clapped her hands, and pointed to us. "How's that? That's the way they do it over at the Cotton Club and the Savoy." She sat down. "My friend Charlie takes the train down to Harlem. He and I go see bands perform at the Savoy and dance all night. We've performed on street corners in Yonkers. Maybe you've seen us?"

"Wow," I said. "That was amazing. I know you

want to be a dancer but your voice is what's going to make you famous. That's why you gotta stay here in Harlem. You can't go to Chicago. You just can't!"

Parker covered my mouth. "Sorry, Ella. Chloe has a pretty good imagination."

Ella rubbed her chin. "If she stops talkin' nonsense, I'll get you food. Won't be much but it'll stop that belly of yours from screamin'."

I pushed Parker's hand away. "You're going to sing at the Apollo Theater tomorrow night. And win."

Ella's mouth dropped open. "How did you know I wanted to go to the Apollo?"

"Um, . . . lucky guess?" I said.

She jerked her head. "Why would a dancer with happy feet want to sing on a fine stage like that?"

Parker's stomach growled again.

Ella covered my mouth. "Hush. You talk too much. If you're comin' to find some food with me, you have to stop talkin' your nonsense. Now let's get going before there's no food left."

Parker glared at me. "Don't say another word until after we eat. I'm starving. Got it?"

I nodded.

We followed Ella out the door and made a left. Along the way, Ella stopped on almost every street corner and couldn't help herself from dancing and singing. Her voice rose up and echoed along the busy street as she bopped around the corner. I didn't recognize the songs but it didn't matter. It was almost as if she were making up the words on her own. She was bebopping and scatting for sure. People stopped and smiled and forgot the hard times for a moment. Some folks danced and clapped along with her.

"I'm going to dance my way to stardom," said Ella. "But I sing on the streets 'cause I make more money that way."

As if on cue, a passing man tossed Ella a coin.

"A dime!" she said. "A good start to the evenin'."

"Actually, Ella," I said. "You're going to become a famous singer. Not a dancer. Trust me."

She looked annoyed. "Are you a fortune teller?" She waved me away. "What do you know? My feet can't stop movin'. Dancin' is in my heart. You ever been to the Savoy? Thirty cents gets you in and when I'm there, I dance all night!"

Parker scowled at me. "If your lips don't stop moving, we won't get food."

I pretended to zip my lips.

As we walked across Seventh Avenue and started up 127th Street, we passed two empty storefronts. I stopped to peek inside the second one. All I could see in the darkness behind the glass was a bunch of empty shelves.

"That was a flower shop," said Ella. "Smelled so sweet when you walked by. Not too many people have money to buy flowers these days."

Parker rubbed his stomach. "I'm so hungry, I'd eat a whole bouquet of flowers!"

Ella burst out laughing as she picked up the pace. She pointed to the upcoming intersection. "It's not far once we turn the corner. Tell your stomach to stop makin' that racket."

As we turned the corner, a gust of wind almost knocked me over. I squinted and shielded my eyes from the blowing dust and bumped smack into Ella and Parker. They had come to an abrupt stop. When I lowered my arm, I saw why. Blocking the path in front of us was a large angry looking man in a pinstriped suit and dark glasses. He had his arms folded and it was obvious he wasn't going to let us pass.

All three of us gasped.

"Slatts!"

A THREAT FROM SLATTS

Slatts had a toothpick sticking out of his mouth and a fancy cane with a gold tip in his hand. He chewed on the toothpick and snarled, "Ella, where do you think you're goin'? You ain't goin' anywhere unless it's with me."

He grabbed her arm and pulled her close. Then he thrust his walking stick into the air and pumped it up and down. "Who are these two hooligans?"

"My friends," said Ella. "You don't need to be worryin' 'bout them."

He barked, "What are you doin' up here in Harlem? Who gave you permission to tag along with Ella?"

Parker stepped back as Slatts's ranting grew louder.

"The only thing you're gonna mess with is me,

Slatts McCoy," screamed Slatts. "Why I'll . . ."

Before he could make any more threats, I kicked him as hard as I could in the shin and screamed, "Run, Ella!"

Slatts dropped his cane and doubled over in pain. Ella's eyes grew big as she stood staring at him.

"Follow me," I screamed. "Don't worry about him! He's too big to run after us. He'll never catch us!"

Ella snapped to attention and her feet finally moved. Parker grabbed my hand and I grabbed Ella's. Together, we took off running. We dodged around Slatts as he lunged at us. He stumbled forward and fell onto the sidewalk. We leaped over him and zigzagged past several garbage cans. The sounds of crashing cans and Slatts's screaming were carried by the wind. "You think you can get away from me, Ella? You can't!"

Ella ran along with us until we slowed down to a walk about five blocks away. We were panting and trying to catch our breath. Then Ella threw back her

head and snorted. "Did you see him? Ol' Slatts just got that fine suit of his all covered with garbage!"

I looked over my shoulder to make sure we had lost him. "He looked like a crazy dog."

Ella wasn't worried. "He's always mad at somethin'. If I'm extra nice to him later, he'll be sweet as pie."

"Don't you think he's bad news?" asked Parker. "Why is someone like you hanging out with someone like him?"

"Because she doesn't know who she is yet," I said in a low voice.

"Course I do," said Ella. "I'm Ella Fitzgerald. A poor girl who's goin' to dance my way to stardom. I'll be the leading act at the Savoy someday. Cotton Club too!"

Ella's pace quickened.

"She's dirt poor," I said. "She has no relatives that she can turn to. No home. Nowhere to go. A lot of her friends aren't good for her to be around." I sighed. "She wants to be a dancer but I know what's going to happen to her. I just wish it would happen soon."

Parker shook his head. "We think we know what's going to happen to her. But are we really sure? Sounds like she's leaving Harlem tomorrow. If she goes, she can't sing at the Apollo Theater can she?"

Parker had a point. I just needed a few minutes alone so I could think things through. I started to think that maybe we were sent back in time to help Ella.

Before I could tell Parker what I was thinking, Ella announced, "We're here! This is 138th Street. The Abyssinian Baptist Church. One of the biggest in Harlem." She looked over her shoulder. "As long as Slatts's thugs don't come runnin' after us, we'll be fine in here. Slatts isn't a religious man. Won't step foot inside a church."

"Aren't you worried he's going to hurt you?" I asked.

"Nah. He's takin' a likin' to me. We're movin' to Chicago. I can handle the old goat."

I had one day to stop her from leaving Harlem.

We walked up a small cobblestone alley that curved around to the back of a large, gray stone and brick church. A sign hanging on a red door said All Are Welcome, All are Loved.

"All but Slatts," I muttered.

When Ella pushed open the door, we could hear the church organ playing and a chorus of people singing hymns.

Ella squeezed past the people by the door. I noticed right away that Parker and I were the only white people there. Some people stared at us until Ella waved them away. "They're with me. They just need some food to quiet their bellies."

As we headed down a narrow flight of stairs, I could smell a wonderful aroma drifting up the stairs.

"Soup's cookin'," said Ella. "If my nose knows, I'd say it's pea soup."

When we got to the last step, it opened up into a huge room. It was packed with people of all ages, shapes and sizes. Many were lined up in front of a long silver counter waiting to be served. Small groups of people were huddled around each other looking tired and worn while little kids raced around.

There was a kitchen with a large stove on the far left side of the room. I could see steam boiling up from the huge pots on the stove. Long tables were hastily set up in the center of the room with different kinds of chairs spread out around them. Some chairs were metal and some were wood but all of them had some sort of tape or rope holding them together.

Two women with white aprons were ladling soup into bowls and handing them to people as they passed by. A reverend in a suit and tie smiled and nodded a blessing to everyone as he plunked a piece of bread right into their soup bowls. Two teenagers with soup-stained aprons were collecting empty bowls from the tables and bringing them back to the kitchen area.

On the other side of the room, I noticed more tables. These were piled high with clothing. Signs over the tables said Mens, Womens, and Child-Sized. Shoes of all sizes were neatly lined up underneath the tables. A mother and two small children were rummaging through the piles and holding up shirts and sweaters to check sizes. An older man was trying on a long winter coat.

"All these people need help?" I said. "That's sad."

"I guess that's why it's called the Great Depression," whispered Parker.

Ella stared at the crowd and touched her heart. "This church has been a real blessin' for most of us here. This is the place to go when there is no place to go. Soup's not bad and the bread's good for dunkin'."

A minute later, a crying child walked up to Ella and held her hands up in the air. Ella swooped her up. "I know the perfect nursery rhyme to dry those tears, Janie. A tisket, a tasket, a green and yellow basket . . ."

Janie kept crying.

"That nursery rhyme is going to be her first number one hit," I said to Parker.

He laughed. "Janie hates it."

And on cue, Janie's crying got even louder.

"Sing it to her, Ella," I said.

Ella looked confused. "It's not a song. Just a rhyme my mama said to me when she tucked me in."

"Sing it," I repeated.

Ella started to sing it slowly.

"Jazz it up, Ella. Make it your own."

On cue, Ella did it! She sang the jazziest version I ever heard. "It's just like her number one hit," I said to Parker.

Janie stopped crying. Ella continued belting it out until a woman rushed over to them.

"Sorry, Ella. Janie's been so cranky today."

Ella kissed the girl's forehead and handed her back to her mother. "Any time, Mrs. Jenkins. She ain't cranky now."

"One day, you're going to be famous for that song," I said.

"It's a silly nursery rhyme," said Ella.

"It *was* a silly nursery rhyme," I said. "But you just turned it into your first number one hit."

She chewed on her lip for a second. "I'm just tryin' to decide if you're just a silly girl or a straight out crazy one." Then she spun on her heels and walked over to the table labeled Mens and picked up a pair of boots. Then she looked us up and down and curled her lip. "My clothes aren't fancy but at least they're warm. I ain't got the notion to say what you're both wearin' but there are clothes over there for the pickin'. Free of course."

She slipped off her worn-out shoes and slid her feet into the boots. "I suppose these boots are for men but they fit me fine." She quickly laced them up.

I remembered that some of the top music men wouldn't hire Ella because she looked too much like a boy so I grabbed some pretty shoes from under the table. "These are nice shoes. Women's shoes."

Ella turned her nose up in the air. "They're pretty. But with winter comin', I'm goin' to need warm boots.

These suit me just fine." Then she sighed. "Beggars can't be choosers, you know." She walked up and down the length of the tables to test her new boots out. "Besides, I'll need these in Chicago. Slatts promised me that he'd buy me pretty shoes once we get there. Proper dancin' shoes, too." She clapped her hands. "In just twenty-four hours, I'll be wavin' goodbye to Harlem forever and sayin' hello to The Windy City. Slatts said I won't have to run numbers there. He has a whole bunch of boys already waitin' for him."

"Don't go," I said as I pulled an itchy sweater over my head. "You have to stay in Harlem."

The reverend was heading toward us.

"What I have to do," said Ella. "Is greet Reverend Smith and get some of that soup in my belly."

While Ella greeted Reverend Smith, I marched over to Parker.

"Look at my new clothes," he said. He held up black pants and a ratty old sweater.

"*New* clothes?" I asked. "They look like they're at

least a hundred years old. And they kind of smell."

He pulled the sweater on over his T-shirt. "At least people will stop staring at me. You need some pants." He looked through his pile and handed me a pair.

After I wiggled into them, I pulled him close. "I think I know why we're here."

Parker raised his eyebrows. "Here in this church or here in Harlem?"

"Both," I said. "You may think I'm crazy but in every time travel book I've ever read, people are always sent back in time to make something right or to make sure someone makes the right choices in their life. Maybe we're here to help Ella."

"Ella?" asked Parker.

I nodded. "She's about to leave for Chicago. If she leaves, she'll miss her shot at the Apollo Theater. If she misses that, who knows what will happen to her."

Parker chewed his lip. "So it's up to us to stop her?"

"Yep," I said.

"And if we don't?"

"If we don't, then the world will never know who she was. They won't be able to hear her amazing voice, see her perform, or be inspired by her.

"Well, we can't change the course of history on an empty stomach," Parker said. "Let's get some soup."

Ella's voice made people happy. People like Mom! If Ella doesn't become a singer, then when we get home to the future, it will be like she never existed. All the lives she touched over the years . . . no one will ever know her as the Queen of Jazz. We couldn't let that happen!

I followed Parker over to the soup line.

A PLACE TO SLEEP

"You gotta place to sleep?" asked Ella as we left the church.

Parker rubbed his eyes. "Nope. We weren't planning on being here tonight."

Ella looked surprised. "Well where did ya think you were goin' to be? It's gettin' late. Ya gotta sleep."

I shrugged.

"Want me to show you where I sleep? There's enough room for all of us. Should be anyway."

"Where is it?" I asked.

But Ella wasn't listening. She pulled a suitcase out from under one of the tables. "Reverend Smith saved this for me on account I'll be needin' it when I go to Chicago."

I pulled Parker aside. "Listen, it's dark out. Mom

must be worried sick about us. I'm worried about us. I know we can't stay here forever, but there's no way I'm walking around here at night trying to find our way back to Bakersfield." I glanced at Ella. "I think we should go with her. She got us food so far. Kept us safe."

Parker exploded. "Safe? She almost got us killed! Slatts might be looking for her. Do you really want to come face to face with him again?"

I grabbed his hands and squeezed them. "I don't ever want to see him again. But I also don't want Ella to either. If we leave now, she'll be in Chicago tomorrow night. We have to make sure she sings at the Apollo Theater at nine o'clock. Sharp!"

"I wanna leave now," said Parker. "I don't want to still be here tomorrow night. I miss being home. I miss Mom. And my friends. Our kitchen. My own bed in my own room. I miss everything!"

"But if we leave now, Ella will go to Chicago and then we'll be stuck here. Forever."

"Forever?" asked Parker.

"Forever," I repeated. "Once we make sure Ella sings at the Apollo, we'll be able to travel back to the future. I can just feel it. Yep. Ella's our ticket back to Bakersfield."

Ella motioned for us as she poked her head outside the door. Once the coast was clear, she burst through the doors and danced her way into the night air.

It wasn't long before we came to a narrow alley between two buildings.

"By comin' in this way," said Ella, "No one will know we're here."

I was pretty sure she was referring to Slatts.

The alley was crowded with stacks of wooden boxes, empty bottles, and a line of overflowing garbage cans. The cans looked as if they had been picked through by stray animals or hungry people. There was an old wooden shed without a door that separated the two buildings.

"Are we sleeping in there?" I said, as I pointed to

the shed. It sure didn't look big enough for all of us.

Ella folded her arms. "No way. Mr. Gulliver got a new freezer last month. Parts of the old ones are in there." She motioned for us to follow her and stopped at two doors leading down to a cellar. "We're sleepin' down there."

Parker and I stared at each other.

"Did you say Mr. Gulliver?" asked Parker

Ella smiled. "I sure did. The one and only. Why? Know him?"

"Sort of," Parker said. "We met him today. In fact, he gave us a message for you."

Ella looked annoyed. "Why didn't you say so? What did he say?"

I took a deep breath. "His exact words were, 'If you see her again, tell her to stay away from Gulliver's, will you? Tell her I said to stay clear away from my place. It's for her own good. Got it?'"

Ella grinned. "That's good to hear. We'll be safe here tonight."

Parker scratched his head. "But he said to stay away. He sounded mad."

Ella walked over to the shed and reached up over the door. She felt around for something. "Ah, here it is." She held up a key. "Mr. Gulliver keeps an extra key hidden above the broken door."

Parker stammered. "I don't think this is such a good idea. Breaking into someone's place will get us in trouble."

Ella looked confused. "We ain't breakin' in anywhere. Mr. Gulliver put that key there for me. And anyone else who needs a dry place to sleep."

Before I could say anything, she walked over to the cellar entrance. There was a big lock holding two doors together. Ella popped in the key and turned it. "Don't just stand there. Help me open up these doors."

The three of us reached down and pulled the doors open.

"This is where Mr. Gulliver gets his deliveries,"

Ella said. "But it's also where he's been helpin' me and some of the other folks in the neighborhood get some sleep."

"I'm confused," I said to Parker.

Ella chuckled. "Girl. I've only known you a few hours and you seem confused most of the time." Then she bounced down the steps. "It's dark down here. Watch your head now."

I pushed Parker in front of me. We crouched down and lowered our heads as we made our way down the stairs.

Ella felt along the wall. "I know it's here somewhere."

No sooner had she spoken than a single light bulb turned on and lit up the tiny room. It was damp and chilly. There were stacks of boxes and a couple of old pushcarts along one wall. The low ceiling was crisscrossed by pipes that ran in all directions.

Suddenly, Parker screamed. "A rat!" He jumped up onto a box and hit his head on a low-hanging pipe.

"Did you see it scurry over there?" He pointed to a darker part of the basement that extended farther away from the storage area.

"Well there are some smaller guests who sleep down here too," said Ella. "But they don't bother no one!" She spread out her arms. "Welcome to the Hotel Gulliver! It sure ain't no Ritz, but it beats sleepin' on the street!"

I wasn't so sure about that.

Right next to the stairs, there were four metal cots with thin mattresses and folded blankets arranged side by side. Ella ran over and pulled a dangling string above the cots. Another light flickered on.

"That's better," said Ella. "Home, sweet, home. At least for tonight."

"If Mr. Gulliver finds you here, he could have you arrested for trespassing," I said. "He made it clear that he doesn't want you around here."

Ella rolled her eyes. "Mr. Gulliver is the sweetest, kindest man I know. He invited me here. In fact, there

are lots of us who come here when we need a safe place to sleep. Sometimes he leaves us food, too." She rushed over to the desk, peeked in a box, and sighed. "Not tonight."

I scratched my head. Why wasn't she listening to us? She caught me giving Parker a strange look.

"Oh, I know what you're thinkin'. But by Mr. Gulliver tellin' me *not* to come here, he was really sayin' that it was safe to come. You see, sometimes inspectors visit. When they do, he'll say, 'Tell the gang to come.' When we hear that, we stay away. But if we hear him tell us to stay away, we come."

"But why not just tell you the truth?" I asked. "Wouldn't that be easier?"

"Because you never know who's snoopin' 'round listenin' to our conversations. Slatts has men workin' for him. Some of them poke their nose around here thinkin' I may show up."

I thought of the photo I had taken of the picture in the Bakersfield Historical Society. "We saw the sign

Mr. Gulliver has in his window. It says No Colored," said Parker. "That's why we're surprised you'd come here."

Ella sat on a wobbly chair. "Are you sure? Mr. Gulliver doesn't care about skin color. He treats everyone the same."

She tapped her fingers on the desk. "You're not tryin' to start trouble for Mr. Gulliver, are you?"

I fished my cell phone out of my pocket. "Here's the proof. I took a picture of it."

"What kind of fancy camera is that?" asked Ella. She looked like she was afraid to touch it. "Are you rich? I ain't never seen a camera like that." Then she grew quiet as she studied the picture.

"Look at the sign," I said. "Do you see what it says?"

"I see it," said Ella. "I can read, ya know. But it don't prove nothin'. I don't even believe that's a real picture. And I ain't never seen a sign like that in Gulliver's. Never."

"You've been inside?" I asked.

"Sure thing. He never turns anyone away. I have a feelin' you're not gettin' the whole story. Besides, Mr. Gulliver is a good man. If it weren't for him, I probably would have left for Chicago long ago. He helped me survive here in Harlem. I just wish I could help him now that he might be needin' it."

"Help him?" asked Parker. "With what?"

"He's no different than others," said Ella. "Money's tight. Not many people have extra money to buy things from his store these days. I heard him sayin' he thinks his money will run out in about two years if things don't get better. Said he may have to close down his shop. I'd do anything to help him. If I had money, I'd gladly give it to him to repay him for his kindness."

That's when I got an idea! "I know a way you could repay Mr. Gulliver."

"You do?" said Ella. Her eyes lit up. "I'd like that."

"But in order to help him, you can't go to Chicago,"

I said. "At least not yet."

Ella's eyes flashed. "What's Chicago have to do with Mr. Gulliver?"

I crossed my fingers. "Well, if you trust me and believe what I'm about to tell you, and it comes true, then you'll have to agree to stay in Harlem."

"And what if I don't believe you? What if what you say is one big lie?"

"Easy," said Parker. "Then you can move to Chicago with Slatts. We won't try to stop you."

"That's right," I said. "You just can't leave until midnight tomorrow. If what I'm telling you doesn't happen by then, you can pack your bags."

"Midnight tomorrow?" said Ella. "Why?"

"Because you're going to win Amateur Night at the Apollo Theater tomorrow night. I'm not sure what time. And once you win, you're going to have a number one record within the next four years. It'll be the "A-Tisket, A-Tasket" song. Then, you won't need Slatts or anyone else anymore."

Ella sat quietly for a long time. Finally, she whispered. "You're sure I'm goin' to make it big? Make money? From my voice?"

I bobbed my head up and down.

"I've always had a notion that I would be famous someday, ya know. Some folks call it confidence. I call it talent."

"You have both," said Parker.

"And with my money, I'll have enough to help save Mr. Gulliver's store?"

We nodded again.

"Deal," she said. "I think you're both crazy but I can wait until midnight tomorrow. It's just a few extra hours." Then she belly laughed. "It will give me extra time to pack all my worldly possessions!"

I felt a sigh of relief. I finally convinced Ella to stay in Harlem. At least until midnight.

Now if I could only figure out how to get Parker and me out of Harlem and back to Bakersfield.

GULLIVER'S FIVE & DIME

"Rise and shine," sang Ella as she pulled the blanket off of me. "I'm as hungry as a street cat. I'm goin' to get me some food then I'm headin' over to Slatts's place. I gotta keep him happy by gettin' him some bettin' slips."

"No! You have to stay away from him," I warned. "We don't want him grabbing you and heading to Chicago before you have a chance to perform at the Apollo Theater tonight."

"He won't leave before eight o'clock tonight," said Ella as she laced up her work boots. "Too big of a bettin' day for Slatts to leave town before then. He says we're leavin' at eight and I believe him. I'll be back here by noon and hide out until we leave for the Apollo. But I gotta hang with him this mornin'.

If I don't bring him some slips by eleven o'clock, he'll come lookin' for me."

Parker groaned. "My back is killing me."

Ella hushed him. "Stop complainin'. You had a free bed. You were warm and safe. What more did you want?"

"To be in my own bed in Bakersfield," he said too low for Ella to hear.

"I gotta go," said Ella. "Can you two survive without me? I'll be back at noon. Mr. Gulliver won't mind you stayin' here until then."

And with that, she ran up the steps and out the doors.

"I'm scared," said Parker when we were alone. "I've had enough of Harlem. I want to go home." He straightened the cots while I folded the blankets. "What if we're stuck here forever?"

"Don't think like that," I said as I put my arm around him. "I've never read a time travel book where the characters got stuck in time. They always get back. Always." He put his head down on the desk. "I think we'll be heading back to Bakersfield tonight. Right after Ella wins."

I shoved my hands behind my back and crossed my fingers. Again.

We walked back to the New Amsterdam Old Dutch Historical Society and found some fresh cookies on the plate. "It's better than nothing," I reminded Parker. "And it's warm in here."

After we got bored looking around, Parker had an idea. "Let's go visit Mr. Gulliver's store."

We walked back and stood in front of the store for a few minutes. The front was painted a cheery red that made it stand out from the other buildings and stores along 123rd Street. The striped red and white canvas awning looked like a candy cane. Large red letters spelled out Gulliver's above the awning. Below it read Five & Dime in yellow.

The front windows were decorated for the season. Thanksgiving candles, plastic turkeys, salt and pepper shakers, and even some pots and pans dotted the window.

"Are you sure you want to go into a place that only allows white people inside?" I asked. "What if Ella has Mr. Gulliver all wrong? What if he really is racist?"

Parker opened the door. "There's only one way to find out."

As we entered the store, I noticed a long counter on the right with a dozen or so swivel seats in front of it. A tired-looking woman stood by a huge cash register that sat on the far end of the counter. Large glass jars full of licorice, gumdrops, sour balls, and lollipops were lined up near the register. Across the room a big brown barrel marked Root Beer perched on a shorter counter.

Behind the long counter was a large mirror with Welcome To Gulliver's painted on it. A couple of signs taped to the mirror said Egg Creams 3¢ and Ice Cream Cones 5¢. On each side of the mirror, glass shelving was neatly stacked with mugs. The store smelled like cotton candy and popcorn. It was much more welcoming than the dank cellar.

Along the floor between the two counters were racks and bins loaded with all kinds of neat things: small tools, soap, combs and brushes, notebooks and pencils, small dolls, bubble gum, toy airplanes, and whistles.

"Wow," Parker said. "Look at all the cool stuff! And everything only costs a nickel or a dime!"

At the center of the store sat a large table with Thanksgiving decorations displayed neatly on top. There were cardboard cutouts of turkeys and pilgrims. A sign said 3¢ Apiece.

As we browsed through the aisles of greeting cards and wrapping paper, Parker pointed to the back of the store where a large popcorn machine on a cart was slowly spewing out popcorn. A man wearing a checkered apron was scooping it into small bags.

When he caught me looking at him, he smiled.

"You two look like you might be heading up to the Majestic to see a movie. Care for some popcorn?"

Parker grabbed my arm and whispered, "It's Mr. Gulliver. He doesn't recognize us."

"We don't have any money for popcorn," I said. "But thanks for asking."

He grabbed two bags and walked toward us. "By the looks of things, I'm guessing you two might be a bit hungry." He held out the bags. "For free."

"Would you give two black kids free popcorn?" I asked.

I heard Parker suck in his breath. "Not again, Chloe. Be quiet."

Mr. Gulliver stood with his hands on his hips and stared at us. He slowly shook his head from side to side. "What kind of question is that?"

I didn't back down. "One that needs an honest answer."

Mr. Gulliver sat down on one of the swivel stools and turned around. "My generosity costs my business a lot of money. But it's just the way I am. I don't care what color a person's skin is. If I see someone in need of food, clothing, or shelter, I give what I can. I'm of the belief that when you do good for people, then they will repay the kindness shown to them by being kind to others."

I suddenly felt two inches tall. "I should have believed Ella. I'm sorry."

"Ella's a friend of yours? Well any friends of Ella's are friends of mine." He extended his hand to Parker and shook it.

I was about to tell him about Slatts's plans when some guy walked into the store lugging a suitcase.

"Daniel! So sorry I'm late," said the man as he set the suitcase down.

Mr. Gulliver shook the man's hand. "You're not late at all. I just finished cleaning your room. Perfect timing. It's great to see you again."

Mr. Gulliver turned toward us. "Kids, this here is a good friend of mine. Name's Frank J. Wilson."

Parker's mouth dropped open. "Did you say Frank J. Wilson?"

The man nodded.

"I thought you looked familiar," said Parker. "You're a legend."

I had no idea who this guy was but Parker sure seemed impressed.

The man winked at Mr. Gulliver. "I told you I was a celebrity. Why just yesterday I was asked for an autograph. Can you imagine?"

Mr. Gulliver got a good laugh. "And just for doing your job? Doing the right thing. Go figure."

"Al Capone was one of the worst thugs I had ever come across," said the man.

"Al Capone?" I asked. "The gangster?"

"The one and only," said Mr. Gulliver. "Mr. Wilson here is one smart man. With all the illegal things Capone did, Mr. Wilson was able to send him to jail for tax evasion."

"And Capone wasn't too happy about it," said the

man. "He's at Alcatraz now and I hear he's not too happy serving his eleven-year sentence there."

"That's why every thug and hooligan from Chicago to the east coast runs scared when they hear your name," said Mr. Gulliver.

The men walked away and sat down in the swivel seats.

"Wow!" I said. "I'm impressed you knew all about him and Capone."

Parker's face turned red. "Actually, I had no idea he was the one who put Al Capone behind bars."

"But you said you knew who he was."

Parker's eyes lit up. "He doesn't know it yet, but he's going to be responsible for convicting someone else just as famous as Capone."

"Who?" I asked.

"Bruno Hauptmann, the Lindbergh Baby kidnapper. In two years, anyone in America who hasn't heard of Mr. Wilson will know his name."

"How did you know about it?"

"I learned about it during my class trip."

I pretended to faint. "Don't tell me! You went to the Bakersfield Historical Society?"

"Nope. We went to the Hunterdon County Courthouse in Flemington, NJ. There's the old courthouse there where they had the 'Trial of the Century.' He proved that the kidnapper was guilty. Of course that part of history hasn't happened yet here." He sighed. "It's tough, isn't it?"

"What's tough?" I asked.

"Being in the past and having to keep your mouth shut when you know what's coming up in the future."

"Yep," I said. "It is hard."

But at this moment, we were dealing with something much harder than having to keep our mouths shut. We still had to figure out a way to get back to Bakersfield.

MISSING ELLA

"Something's wrong," I said. "She should have been here by now." I glanced at my watch. "She said she'd meet us here at noon. It's already one o'clock."

Parker felt for the key above the shed's door. "I'm not waiting out here any longer. It's freezing. Mr. Gulliver leaves the key for people who need it. Let's face it. We need it."

Within a minute, we were back inside the musty cellar.

"Do you think she's okay?" I asked. "Where could she be?"

"I'm sure she's fine," said Parker. "She's used to roaming around. She doesn't know us that well. I doubt she's sitting somewhere thinking about us."

"What if she's with Slatts?"

"Chloe! Come on! You know she's with him. She told us she was going to see him today. I'm sure she'll be back any minute."

We found a deck of cards and played Go Fish for a while. Then I couldn't take it anymore. "What if she left for Chicago already? Or what if Slatts has her and won't let her go?"

Parker looked at my watch. "We have about eight hours to find her." He paced back and forth. "If we don't find her, does it mean we're stuck here forever?"

"I'm not sure," I said. Then I plopped down on a cot and cried. "I wish Mom were here. She'd know what to do."

Parker sat next to me. "I know Mom's not here but I think I know someone who can help us."

"Mr. Gulliver?" I asked as I wiped my nose.

Parker nodded. "And Mr. Wilson, too."

A minute later, we were standing in front of Gulliver's. Mr. Gulliver and Mr. Wilson were sitting at the counter eating lunch. I burst through the door. "Ella needs your help. We need your help."

Mr. Gulliver looked concerned. "Is Ella in trouble? I help her as much as I can but she hides things from me. She knows I don't approve of her relationship with Slatts."

Mr. Wilson looked up from his plate. "Slatts? Slatts McCoy?"

I nodded. "That's him! Do you know him?"

He wiped his mouth then threw the napkin on his plate in disgust. "He's Al Capone's friend. He used to live in Chicago and did some of Capone's dirty work for him. He's a thug all right. But not nearly as dangerous as Capone."

"We think he has Ella," I said. "They're supposed to leave for Chicago today. But Ella decided she wasn't going. She had to go over to his place today but promised she'd be back at noon. But she's not here. We even checked the cellar."

"My cellar?" asked Mr. Gulliver. "Did Ella show

you where the key is hidden? Have you two been staying there?"

I nodded. "Ella said you wouldn't mind."

Mr. Gulliver looked at his watch. "Two hours late? Now I'm worried about her."

He turned to Mr. Wilson. "Ella's only seventeen. Doesn't have any family she can count on. But she can dance and sing with the best of them. I'm convinced she's going to be famous one day."

"She is," I said. "In fact, we know she's going to be famous. Sooner than you think."

Mr. Wilson laughed. "You know she's going to be famous?" He took a sip of his milkshake. "My, my, my. You two are certainly smart cookies."

He didn't believe us.

Parker looked mad. "Yes, Mr. Wilson. We know that Ella is going to be famous one day. In fact, she's going to win Amateur Night at the Apollo Theater tonight if we can get her there."

Mr. Wilson sat there with a smirk on his face.

That made Parker's face even redder than it already was. "In less than five years, she'll have a number one hit record and be richer than anyone you know. You'll see." Then he softened his voice. "But we need both of you to help us find her today so we can make sure she'll perform tonight."

Mr. Wilson snorted. "Sorry. My help is reserved for the United States Government." He turned to Mr. Gulliver. "There's no way these kids can know those things." He faced Parker. "What you meant is that you *hope* she does those things. You're not fortune tellers."

"Wrong again," said Parker. "As a matter of fact, we do know it. Just like we know that when Charles Lindbergh's baby was kidnapped, you insisted that the serial numbers on the ransom money be recorded. Because of you, Bruno Hauptmann was arrested for the kidnapping."

I high-fived Parker. "Impressive!"

Mr. Wilson's face twitched. He looked around

the store nervously. "How do you know that? No one knows that except some of my government friends in Jersey."

Parker shrugged his shoulders. "We just know these things, Mr. Wilson."

Mr. Wilson straightened himself up. "Okay, kid you're giving me the willies. I don't know how you know these things but I believe you." He rubbed his chin for a minute. "Alright, if you want my help, I'll be happy to provide it."

Mr. Gulliver agreed. "Of course I'll help find Ella. And if she's singing at the Apollo Theater tonight, you better believe I'll be there to watch her."

After searching around Harlem for the next several hours, we never found Ella. She found us!

We were crossing Lenox Avenue when Slatts's tan car stopped at the light. I recognized it right away. "Parker, isn't that Slatts's car?"

Just then, the window rolled down and Ella popped her head out and waved. "Chloe! Parker!"

"It's Ella," I shouted as I ran toward the car. A truck was in front of the car and a car was in back blocking it in. It had nowhere to move.

I opened the door. "Come on, Ella. We have to get you ready for the Apollo."

But Ella didn't budge. Slatts was the one who stepped out of the car. "You two hooligans again? She ain't goin' anywhere with you kids. We're headin' out to Chicago. We're done with Harlem and movin' on to bigger and better."

"I don't think Ella wants to go with you," I said.

This made Slatts slap his thigh and laugh. "Since when does she have a choice?"

Ella leaned out the window again. "I told you he wouldn't leave me behind. He heard me talkin' to a friend about singin' at the Apollo tonight and said he wouldn't allow it. Said I make money for him and only him."

"He's not the boss of you," said Parker.

Slatts moved toward me. "Actually, I am the boss

of Ella. She's my girl. Whatcha gonna do about it? Kick me again?" This time, he laughed so hard he bent over to catch his breath.

Slatts was obviously enjoying this conversation.

Until Mr. Wilson walked up and tapped him on the shoulder!

Slatts swatted the hand off of his shoulder and swung around. "Who's touchin' my new suit? I'll ..."

When he saw Mr. Wilson, his eyes grew wide. He gulped and took three steps back.

"Remember me, Slatts? By the look on your face, I'd say you do. In fact, your ears must have been ringing because I just visited Al Capone at Alcatraz last week. Had to settle some business. Guess what I told him? I said it was *you* that told me where he kept his books."

Slatts dropped his walking stick. "It wasn't me! Why'd you go and tell him that? He'll find a way to even the score from jail. You gotta set the record straight."

"Really?" said Mr. Wilson. "I must have a foggy

memory. Doesn't matter really because if you don't let Ella go, I'm going to launch an investigation into your businesses. Then I'll arrest and convict you Capone style. And when the judge asks where I want you to serve your time, you know what I'm going to say?"

"What?" I asked.

"I'm going to say, 'Put him in Capone's cell in Alcatraz.' That's what I'm going to say."

Slatts looked terrified. "He'll kill me. You can't do that." He started to cry like a baby.

"I can and I will," said Mr. Wilson. "Unless you leave Ella here and get out of Harlem right now and never look back. If you don't, you can be sure I'll hunt you down."

Slatts didn't have to think twice about it. He tipped his hat to Ella. "No woman is worth going to Alcatraz for."

He opened the car door for Ella and as she stepped out, he stepped back in and sped away.

And that's the last we ever saw of Slatts McCoy.

CHAPTER 8

ELLA SINGS

Mr. Gulliver stopped his car in front of the Apollo Theater at seven o'clock. "Mr. Wilson and I will be back at nine o'clock. Sharp!"

Ella slid over and opened the door. Before she got out, she blushed. "You're all makin' such a fuss over my singin' here tonight. I hope I don't disappoint."

Parker and I got out the other side. "Trust me," I said. "You won't disappoint anyone. The audience is gonna love you!"

Ella stepped out of the car in her clunky men's boots. "I better get in there. Don't want them starting without me."

Mr. Gulliver honked his horn as he drove away.

I couldn't help staring at Ella's boots. I groaned. "Are you sure you can't wear a pair of women's shoes?"

"These are fine," she said as she ducked inside a stage door and waved good-bye. "Stop frettin'."

"Good luck," I yelled. But the door had already closed.

"She doesn't need luck," said Parker. "Does she? We know she wins."

"As long as she sings, she'll win," I said. "But I'm worried she'll try to dance."

Parker looked down. "I'm just worried we won't get back to Bakersfield."

I squeezed his hand and led him to the end of the line. It stretched across the sidewalk and rounded the corner. It was freezing! The wind whipped through the buildings and blew bits of paper all around Harlem.

Parker's teeth chattered. He tried to pull up the collar of his ratty sweater. "Man, I miss my hoodie."

On the corner, there were two men entertaining the crowds. One was playing a saxophone and another was strumming an old bass. It sounded smooth and peaceful even above the constant honking of horns and the grinding of the traffic on the street.

The line moved briskly. We got through the main doors and into the lobby with twenty minutes to spare.

The first thing I noticed were the brightly lit chandeliers hanging from the high ceilings. "I can't believe we're actually in the Apollo Theater," I said. "I wish Mom were here." We hurried past the staircases that led up to the balconies. An usher looked at us a bit skeptically.

"If you hurry, there are still seats in the orchestra but they're filling fast." Then he looked around trying to see if anyone else was with us. "You got parents with you?"

"No," said Parker. "Our cousin is performing."

That was good enough for the usher. He tipped his hat to us and smiled. "Good luck!"

We made our way through the glass doors and stopped to take in the sight. The stage was down below us and two balconies were up above us. Behind us, there were more balconies that hung from each side of the stage. They were already jam-packed with people.

It was loud and getting rowdy. The house band was warming up the crowd. Two men in tuxedoes were standing toward the front of the stage carefully looking over pages in a notebook. Finally, the main show started. The hour flew by. We sat back and listened to some comedians tell jokes and heard the Benny Carter Orchestra play. Then, the famous Edwards Sisters, a tap dancing duo, took the stage. They brought down the house with an amazing performance. The main show ended at nine o'clock.

"Where's Ella?" I asked. "Do you see her?"

Parker pointed to the right side of the stage.

"OMG!" I said. "She's first in line. I think she might be first!"

Even from the distance, I could tell that Ella looked as nervous as I felt. By her appearance, she didn't look like she had a chance of winning. She wore a tattered and faded dress and threw on a light blue sweater over it. The elbows on the sweater were ripped. She paced back and forth in her clunky boots and her hair was a mess. As usual.

"She looks awful," I said to Parker. "No matter what I said, I couldn't convince her to run a comb through her hair or change out of those boots."

"Does it matter?" said Parker. "You know she wins anyway."

But it did matter! I knew that her appearance would cost her the customary week-long gig at the theater that came with the prize money.

"Ladies and gentlemen," boomed a voice. "Amateur Night will begin in two minutes."

The crowd went wild. Some crazy guy dressed like a skeleton whipped the crowd into a frenzy on the other side of the stage. He jumped all around and pointed to Ella who was standing at the other end.

"Who's that man?" I asked the woman next to me.

"Everyone knows who that is. It's Porto Rico." She laughed. "If we boo the performer off the stage, he comes and gets 'em! He'll chase them clear out of this theater. If any of these amateurs think they can dance like the Edwards Sisters, Porto Rico will sweep 'em away with that broom of his."

Parker laughed. But I suddenly had an awful feeling inside my stomach. "We have to make sure Ella sings," I shouted. "We have to get Ella's attention."

The theater was filled to the rafters. The air was electric. The crowd was ready to roar. The place was hot. Sweltering. Most people were standing and ready for the amateurs to take the stage. The band played a jazzed-up swing tune and some younger people danced in the aisles. One of the men in a tuxedo walked toward the center of the stage and the band stopped playing. The crowd got even louder. The woman next to me jumped up and whistled.

The man who approached the microphone was the master of ceremonies.

"Ladies and gentlemen, welcome to Amateur Night at the Apollo Theater!"

The crowd roared once again before finally quieting down.

"Now folks," said the man. "You know how it works. If you like what you hear, let us know it with your applause. If not well . . . you know what to do!"

A thunderous roar filled the room.

Just then, Porto Rico pounced onstage waving and twirling a broom. He started moving his arms back and forth in a sweeping motion.

"We all know what he means by that," said the man in the tuxedo. "If the boos win out, the performer will get swept right off this stage!"

Another wave of hooting and hollering.

Finally, the crowd settled down.

"Tonight's prize is ten dollars and a stint at the Apollo next week. Winner takes all. Losers go home!"

I could see Ella standing all alone. "She has to sing, Parker. I'm going to tell her again. No dancing!"

I jumped out of my seat and despite the crowd spilling into the aisle, I was able to make my way down to the stage. On the way, I saw Mr. Gulliver and Mr. Wilson in the crowd. I waved at Ella to get her attention.

When she saw me, her trembling hands flashed a little piece of paper. It read #1. I was right! She was going on first! Even from twenty feet away, I could see the fear in her face. She even looked wobbly in those sturdy boots. She mouthed "Edwards Sisters" and then, "I think I'll dance."

Dance! "No, Ella! Don't dance," I shouted. But the emcee walked up to the group and started talking to the performers. I could barely see her now.

I waved my arms frantically. "Ella, Ella!" She leaned back and her eyes briefly caught mine. She smiled nervously and raised her eyebrows as if to say "wish me luck."

I pointed to my mouth and yelled, "Sing! You have to sing! Do not dance!"

But the emcee took her arm to lead her to the stage.

I rushed back to Parker and fell into my seat.

Twenty seconds later, Ella was introduced. She stumbled out to the center of the stage. The lights made her appearance even worse. If she wasn't wearing a dress, most people would have thought she was a man.

"Ladies and gentlemen, this is Ella Fitzgerald." The crowd let out a groan mixed with laughter.

"Ella is going to da . . ."

Maybe it was my suggestion. Or maybe she made up her own mind. But before the man could say the word *dance,* Ella held up her hand to stop him. He walked over to her and she whispered in his ear.

He pointed back toward the orchestra and Ella turned around to face the band. The saxophonist leaned over. Ella took a few steps toward him and spoke. The restlessness was taking over the crowd. They started to voice their opinions.

"What ya gonna do?"

"Ha! What are you dressed as? The wash lady?"

"Get out the broom!" yelled a man.

The emcee's voice finally boomed through microphone. "Ella's going to sing us 'Judy'."

Parker and I probably didn't realize it since we were too caught up in the moment, but history was being made.

The audience was rowdy. To quiet them down, the orchestra started playing.

Parker looked nervous. "This audience is really tough. Did you hear what they're shouting at Ella?"

I crossed my fingers and closed my eyes as Ella stepped up to the microphone. Finally, she started to sing.

"If her voice can bring
Every hope of spring
That's Judy, My Ju–"

Her voice cracked! It sounded like she had forgotten the lyrics. She looked nervous and not at all confident. The crowd started to rumble with deafening boos and laughter.

"This can't be happening," Parker moaned.

"It'll be okay," I said. "Promise."

Even though I knew what would happen next, I was still nervous. The audience wanted her to be swept off the stage and were calling Porto Rico's name.

"Go back to the street!" someone shouted.

"Come back when you know what you're doin'!" yelled a man from the balcony.

Just then, the announcer took a few steps to the front and put his hand up in the air. He motioned for the band to stop. He smiled at Ella and took the microphone from her. Ella took a deep breath and stepped a few feet back from the front of the stage.

The man calmed the crowd down. "Hold on a second, folks. This girl has a gift and just needs to take a moment so she can unwrap it. Let's start it again, shall we?"

Ella turned and said something to the orchestra. The announcer gave the microphone back to Ella and once again, the orchestra began to play. This time, it was a different song.

I knew it right away. It was a song that would one day be sung by one of Ella's favorite singers, Connie Boswell. My mom had it on one of her records. It was "The Object of My Affection".

Ella closed her eyes and just as the audience started to get loud again, she sang with all her heart.

> *"The object of my affection*
> *Can change my complexion*
> *From white to rosy red ...'*

By the time she finished the third line the audience was dead silent. Mesmerized. There was no doubt of her ability now. Ella's voice was smooth as silk. Smooth and in tune. She was a natural singer and appeared totally confident despite her raggedy appearance.

"Wow," whispered Parker. "Just wow!" He turned to face me. "Now I get it. I know why you and Mom love her so much. Her voice is smooth like velvet."

People all around us were nodding their heads in approval. As Ella finished the song, the master of ceremonies came forward and smiled ear to ear. The audience erupted into applause. Some gave Ella a standing ovation as she shyly waved to the audience and quickly left the stage to a thunderous roar of approval.

"That. Was. Amazing," I said.

"I can't believe she can sing like that!" Parker said looking excited. It sounded like one of Mom's records being played."

We sat back in our seats and watched the rest of the show. A lot of the singers and dancers were good, but I think everyone knew that Ella had set the tone for the rest of the night.

By the end of the hour, all of the amateurs had performed. Anyone who wasn't booed off the stage earlier was called back onstage one last time to see who would get the loudest applause from the audience.

All of the performers received applause but when Ella was introduced again, the audience went crazy! Ella won by a landslide.

"This is just so amazing!" I said to Parker after screaming our approval as well. "I can't believe we saw this moment."

Parker pinched me.

"Ouch! What did you do that for?"

"Just in case you were going to ask me to do it!"

We both laughed like crazy.

"Mom would have loved it," he said. "I miss her."

"I miss her, too," I whispered.

Even though we just saw something amazing happen, and even though I knew that we might have had something to do with it, I couldn't stop thinking about Mom. It made me homesick, and, for a moment, I wondered if we would ever get back home.

CHAPTER
9

THE SIGN IN THE WINDOW

"To Ella," said Mr. Gulliver as he raised his root beer float in the air. "You were magnificent."

"I thought we were going to be late," said Mr. Wilson. "It's a good thing we got there on time since Ella went on first."

We clinked glasses.

"I told you that you'd win," I said. "I'm just so glad that Slatts wasn't able to get you to Chicago."

"Who?" said Ella. She let out a hoot and a holler. She raised her float again. "I should be toastin' all of you. If it weren't for Parker and Chloe, I wouldn't be sittin' here with ten dollars in my pocket."

"Or a week-long singing gig at the Apollo next week," said Mr. Gulliver.

Parker and I looked at each other.

"Tell her," said Parker.

"Tell me what?"

I took a deep breath. "I stand by everything I said to you about winning Amateur Night at the Apollo Theater, Ella. You are going to be a rich and famous singer."

Ella bit her lip. "But?"

"But you're not going to be singing at the Apollo next week," said Parker.

"Don't be silly," said Ella. "Course I am. That's the prize, ain't it?" She looked from me to Parker to Mr. Gulliver and then finally, her eyes landed on Mr. Wilson.

Mr. Wilson shrugged. "Don't ask me. Ask them." He pointed to Parker and me. "Those two seem to know *everything*."

"Give me the truth," said Ella. "I can handle it."

"Okay," I said. "They're gonna tell you that your voice was as smooth as silk. That they never saw the audience react to anyone the way they did to you."

"What's so bad about that?" asked Ella.

"But then they'll tell you that they don't think you look like you belong on the Apollo's stage. Your hair's a mess. Your clothes aren't right." I pointed to her boots. "And those clunky things? They gotta go."

"So they think I'm ugly?" asked Ella. She smiled shyly. "I can polish up real nice if I want to. I guess I just didn't see any need to. But, if that's what they want, then that's what I'm gonna give them." She sighed. "Funny how it wasn't the color of my skin that's keepin' people from wantin' to work with me. It was just the sight of me."

I hugged her tight. "Don't worry about the Apollo Theater. Now that you've won, people will hear all about you. Pretty soon, you'll be singing with a guy named Duck . . . Duck something."

"Duck? I don't know any Duck." Then her eyes lit up. "You don't mean *Chick* do you? Chick Webb?"

"That's it!" I slapped my forehead. "Chick. Not duck." I flashed a smile. "Sorry about that! It won't be long before you win Amateur Night at the Harlem Opera House too. In fact, you're going to win every amateur night you enter. That's a lot of money! After that, the sky's the limit."

"And when exactly am I gonna have that number one record you told me about?" she asked.

"In 1938. Just four years from now," I said. "You'll only be twenty-one years old!"

"That's still just a baby," said Mr. Wilson.

"Just remember to make that nursery rhyme as jazzy as you can." I said. "Just like when you sang it to Janie."

Ella got up and twirled around the store as she sang the song.

"A-Tisket, a-tasket, a green and yellow basket.
I sent a letter to my mommy and on the way I
dropped it . . ."

She beamed. "I may change the colors. You know, to make it my own." Then she treated us to a concert of her favorite songs and we danced around the store.

The others were still dancing when Parker pulled me aside.

"We're still here," he said in a voice so low I could hardly hear him. "I thought we'd be back in Bakersfield by now."

So did I. But I didn't want to get Parker any more upset than he already was. "I'm sure it's just a matter of time. I mean, we changed history. We made things right, didn't we?"

Before he had time to answer, Ella belted out a new tune. She sang her own jazzy version of "Happy Birthday" to Mr. Gulliver.

After she finished, Mr. Wilson pulled a cake out from behind the counter. "Can't celebrate without a cake now, can we?"

"Happy birthday, Mr. Gulliver," I said.

"Yeah, happy birthday," said Parker. "I hope you get to do something you like." He shot me a look.

Then Ella slid a card over to Mr. Gulliver. "It's an IOU, Mr. Gulliver. When my money comes in, I'm gonna give you a big chunk of it. I want to repay your kindness. And you didn't just help me. You helped everyone who needed a dry place to sleep and food in their bellies."

Mr. Gulliver picked up the card and read it. His eyes watered.

"Don't you be gettin' all misty-eyed over an IOU," said Ella.

Mr. Gulliver turned the card over for us to see. "It's what she wrote to me that's making my eyes water. It's the nicest letter anyone's ever written."

I took a closer look. It was signed, Love and kisses, Ella Fitzgerald. Amateur Night Winner at the Apollo Theater November 21, 1934.

I handed it to Parker so he could have a look and then I handed Mr. Gulliver a tissue.

"Forget the tissue," said Mr. Wilson. "He needs a party hat."

"The hat!" I shouted.

Parker turned to Ella. "Do you have that purple pillbox hat from yesterday? We sorta need it."

Ella ran down to the cellar and was back in a flash. She plopped it on the table. "You want the ratty ol' thing? You can have it!"

I put the hat gently on my head and waited for the shaking and flashes of light to begin. But nothing happened. I could see the disappointment in Parker's face out of the corner of my eye.

"I wish I had one of those fancy cameras so I could take a picture of this special night," said Mr. Gulliver. "It would make a great memory."

I whipped out my cell phone and powered it up. "It still works!" I said.

"What is that thing?" asked Mr. Wilson.

Parker laughed. "Don't ask. Just trust us and smile."

I pointed to Mr. Gulliver and Ella. "I'll take your pictures first. Let's go outside so I can get the store in the picture too."

We all went out and stood on the sidewalk in front of the store. Mr. Gulliver and Ella stood in front of the window.

"Hold still," I said, focusing the camera. "On the count of three ..."

I was just about to take the picture when I noticed the sign in the window.

"Parker," I said. "Look at the sign over Mr. Gulliver's shoulder."

Parker looked over. "It says, 'No Colored'." He frowned.

Then Mr. Gulliver bent down to tie his shoe and the whole sign was exposed. It said "No Colored *Denied*."

Parker gasped. "He was blocking part of the sign! I knew he was a good guy!"

"I told you not to believe everything you hear," said Ella.

I felt bad for assuming Mr. Gulliver was racist. I turned to him to apologize. As I turned my head, the hat fell to the ground.

"What's all the fussin' 'bout?" asked Ella. "Take the picture already."

I counted, "One, two . . ."

"Wait," said Ella. She leaned down and scooped the hat up and held it over my head. But before she did, she asked me an odd question. "What's your favorite color, Chloe?"

"Yellow," I said.

She turned to Parker. "What's yours?"

"Brown," he said. "Why?"

But she never answered. She simply smiled and slowly lowered the hat onto my head.

In a split second, the light seemed to grow dimmer and the air got cooler. There was a flash of light followed by another and then another.

And then, everything went black.

And we never saw Ella Fitzgerald again.

MAKING IT HER OWN

"Parker? Are you there?" I groaned and rubbed my head. "Where are we?"

"I'm right here," he said.

For a second, Parker's voice sounded like it was in a bottle. But once I shook my head and my ears popped, everything came into focus. "I can smell old newspapers . . ."

"And dirty diapers," Parker whispered.

I sat up. "Does this mean . . . ?"

Parker jumped to his feet. "Yep! We're back in Bakersfield! I think so anyway."

We were adjusting to the light but our senses were telling us that we were in a familiar place once again.

I glanced around the room. "Look at all the concert posters! And the sign says . . ."

"I see it," said Parker. "Bakersfield Historical Society."

Parker and I hugged each other. Then we stood there quietly for a minute to take it all in.

Finally, Parker spoke up. "Yep. We're home." He sounded relieved.

"And the old clothes we had on?" I said looking down. "They're gone!" I rubbed my eyes. "I can't believe we're home. Finally!" That's when I heard it. "Sh. Listen. Do you hear that?"

Parker's eyes widened. A huge smile spread across his face. "I sure do! It sounds like jazz coming from the stage at the festival! And let me tell you something, it's music to *my* ears!" He high-fived me. "We're home, Chloe! Let's go find Mom."

"Wait a minute," I said. "I need time to think about everything." I started to think aloud. "How long were we gone? Was it days? Weeks? Years? What are we gonna find when we open that door? Did it even happen or was I just dreaming?"

Parker bit his lip. "If you were dreaming, then I was dreaming the same dream. We went to *Harlem*, Chloe. In 1934. Back in time! Way, way back in time. We met Ella Fitzgerald and saw her perform at the Apollo Theater! And there was Slatts, the church, and ..."

"Mr. Gulliver and his store," I said. I glanced around the exhibit. "Look, over there. There's the empty shelf that the hat was on." I reached up and lifted Ella's purple pillbox hat off my head and placed it back where it belonged. Then Parker and I carefully hung the posters back up on the wall.

"Looks like it did when we first arrived," I said. We looked around one last time before we headed for the door.

"You go first," Parker said.

"Why, what's wrong?"

Parker spoke softly. "What if we're *not* home in Bakersfield? What if we open the door and we're back in Harlem? Or if we're somewhere else?"

I pushed past him. "Well, there's only one way to find out," I said as I turned the handle and opened the door.

Bright sunshine and blue skies greeted us. "Looks like a beautiful July day," I said.

"No humidity," said Parker. He breathed a sigh of relief.

Music was blasting from the stage. I took a deep breath. "Can you smell all that food?"

On cue, Parker's stomach roared like a lion.

A boy ran past us. "Hey, James! Where's Logan?" Parker shouted.

The boy turned around. "Logan was over on the Green tossing a football around the last time I saw him. I think he was looking for you. If I see him, I'll tell him you're looking for him."

"Thanks!" Parker said. He turned to face me. "So, it's official. We're home!"

I dropped to my knees and kissed the ground. "Let's go find Mom."

We hurried over to the Green and backtracked through the people on blankets and zigzagged through the lawn chairs. There were lots of people dancing.

"They sure can't dance like Ella!" I said.

Parker smiled. "You got that right!"

Once we were in the middle of the Green, we spotted Mom. Parker ran ahead of me and practically tackled her. "Mom! I'm so glad to see you!"

"Me, too!" I said as I wiped my eyes. "I've never been so happy to see anyone before."

"Wow," Mom said. "I'm happy to see you guys too!" She looked us up and down. "Is everything okay? You both seem just a tad bit too excited to see me." She slathered some sunscreen on her arms. "You were gone such a long time for as much as you complained about having to go. Did you find the bathroom?"

I felt my heart race. "How long were we gone?"

Mom looked at her watch. "At least twenty minutes."

Parker's eyes met mine. I leaned into his ear and whispered, "Twenty minutes? That's all?" Then I sat next to Mom. "Were you worried about us?"

"Nah," said Mom giving me a strange look. "Twenty minutes isn't that long. I know how much you like all the artifacts in that building so I figured you were looking through the exhibit. Was I right?"

"Yeah," said Parker. "Something like that."

Just then, we heard a woman start to sing.

"A tisket, a tasket . . ."

"I've always loved this song," said Mom. "Who would have thought a nursery rhyme could have been turned into a number one hit?"

Parker and I smirked. "Not us."

The three of us started singing along to the song as loud as we could. Then Mom held up her hand for us to stop. "I messed up the words. The nursery rhyme says, 'A green and yellow basket' but Ella changed it to 'a brown and yellow basket.'" She scratched her head. "I wonder why?"

Parker's eyes grew wide. Then we both whispered, "She made it her own!"

"You think she did that because of us?" asked Parker.

I thought back to the moment she placed the hat back onto my head.

"Well, I did say my favorite color was yellow."

"And I told her mine was brown," said Parker.

A chill ran up my spine. "We did it, Parker. We changed history. We made it right again. Ella's music is around today because of us."

Parker nodded and plopped down on the lawn.

A few minutes later, Logan ran up to us. "There you are, Parker. I've been looking all over for you. Want to throw the football around?"

Parker looked at Mom and then me. "Sorry. I can't. We're planning our trip to New York next month. We're going to Amateur Night at the Apollo Theater. That's in Harlem, you know."